"THOSE MEN ARE TRYING TO BREAK INTO OUR MINIVAN!" MARY WHISPERED. "WHAT DO WE DO?"

Lucy reached into her purse. "I've got the Mace."

"No," said Mary. "We should call the police. Let them handle it."

"Okay, give me the cell phone," said Lucy.

"I left it in the van!" said Mary.

"There's a pay phone over there," said Lucy. "But those guys will see us if we try to call anybody."

"I'm getting mad now," said Mary. "They have no right—"

She was interrupted by a loud shriek. The girl they'd seen earlier—the one going through the trash cans—was now rushing toward the two guys. She had a thick branch in her hands. She swung it like a club.

"We better help!" Mary cried, rushing forward. . . .

DON'T MISS THESE

7th Heaven

BOOKS!

7th Heaven.

DRIVE YOU CRAZY

by Amanda Christie

An Original Novel

Based on the hit TV series
created by Brenda Hampton

Random House 🏠 New York

www.randomhouse.com/kids

Library of Congress Catalog Card Number: 00-109753
ISBN: 0-375-81159-1

Printed in the United States of America
April 2001
10 9 8 7 6 5 4

7th Heaven.

DRIVE YOU CRAZY

ONE

"Okay, everybody, we're just about ready to take the picture," Mary Camden said.

Peering through the lens of her father's Polaroid camera, Mary moved a bit to the right and then to the left until her sisters and brother were perfectly in the frame.

Lucy, Ruthie, and Simon were all sitting on a bench in the backyard. Behind them, a big tree provided a pretty green backdrop.

"Ready—" she said.

"Wait! Wait a second!" Simon called.

"For what?" asked Mary.

"C'mere, Happy! Come on, girl."

Mary waited patiently as Simon pulled the fluffy white family dog onto his lap.

"That's a good idea," Mary admitted. "Grandpa Charles will remember Happy. Or at least he should. Okay, here we go again."

But this time, Mary stopped herself.

Four pairs of eyes were just staring at her with glassy, distracted expressions. No one was smiling!

"Come on, guys, loosen up," Mary called. "Grandpa Charles is going to think this is a mug shot instead of a family portrait!"

Sighs and grumbles followed. Mary had been trying to get the perfect picture for way too long. But finally, Lucy, Simon, and Ruthie all plastered grins on their faces.

"That's better," Mary said. "Say 'cheese.'"

But just as Mary clicked the picture, Happy sprang from Simon's lap and rushed at the camera, barking.

"Shoo!" Mary cried.

"Whoa! Down, Happy!" Simon called firmly. "Behave yourself, girl."

Happy slithered sheepishly back to Simon's side, her tail between her legs.

"Do you think I got the shot before

Happy moved?" Mary fretted.

Lucy yanked the Polaroid out of the camera and watched as the photo appeared.

She made a face.

"How's it look?" Simon asked.

"Oh, it's a great picture—of Happy's tonsils."

Mary grabbed the photo. The picture was all white teeth and pink tongue—it looked more like an outtake from *Jurassic Park* than a Camden family portrait.

Mary threw the picture on the picnic table. "Okay, everybody into position again. We need another take."

"Yes, Ms. *Spielberg,*" Lucy said with a toss of her head.

As everyone lined up, Mary snapped her fingers in the air.

"Grandpa Charles's memory album: grandkids' photo, take two. Say 'cheese'!"

Once again, Happy rushed the camera.

"What's wrong with Happy?" Mary demanded, throwing up her hands.

"She likes cheese," Ruthie explained. "So when you say 'cheese,' she thinks that there is some cheese to eat and she wants it."

Mary looked incredulous. "Are you telling me that Happy knows what the word 'cheese' means?"

Simon nodded. "Happy has a pretty big vocabulary."

"Yeah," said Ruthie. "And she knows a lot of words, too. Just joking! Get it? It's a redundancy!"

Mary shook her head. Ruthie had recently received a scholarship to an elite private school. Now her head was way too big for her little body. Mary glanced up at the afternoon sky.

"No more jokes, Ruthie. We're losing the sun. Let's try this again."

"But this time, *don't* say 'cheese'!" But when Lucy said the magic word, Happy jumped on her, tail wagging.

"See!" Ruthie cried. "Now Happy thinks *Lucy* has the cheese."

Lucy pushed the dog away and looked at Mary. "You'll just have to say something else."

Mary rolled her eyes.

"But I *always* say 'chee'—you know!" she insisted. "How will anybody know I'm about to take the picture if I don't say—" She glanced down at the dog. Happy's ears were perked up expectantly. "—well, you know?"

"Maybe you should say 'baloney,'" Lucy offered.

Happy ran to Lucy's side and barked.

"She likes baloney, too," Simon told them.

"Come on, guys," Mary said. "This is a photo for Grandpa Charles's memory album, not a major Hollywood production. Let's get this show on the road."

"Maybe we should lose the dog," Lucy whispered to Mary.

"Try saying 'pepperoni,'" Ruthie advised.

Mary blinked.

"It's too spicy," explained Ruthie. "Happy doesn't like pepperoni."

"Good idea," Simon said, patting his sister's head. "Glad to see you're thinking."

Ruthie smiled proudly.

"Places!" Mary cried, pushing Lucy toward the others.

When everybody was ready, Mary peered through the lens.

"Looking good," she whispered. "Now say . . . *'pepperoni'*!"

The shutter clicked and this time

Happy stayed in place. When the photo came out, everyone watched the image automatically develop.

"Perfect!" Mary announced, showing the Polaroid to the others.

"Let's try another pose," said Lucy. "But this time, I'll work the camera and Mary will be in the picture."

"Hey," Simon cried, "I want to take a picture, too!"

"Don't worry. You'll get a turn. . . ."

Mrs. Camden was watching her children through the kitchen window when Reverend Camden came through the back door.

"What's going on?" he asked.

"The kids are finishing up the memory album for Grandpa Charles," Mrs. Camden replied. "This is the last set of photos, and time is running out."

Reverend Camden frowned. "Actually, they may have more time than they thought. There's been a change of plans."

"What's going on?"

"You remember Reverend Devlin, from the Palm Street Church. He was supposed to represent Glenoak at the two-day Family and Church Ministers Conference this weekend, but . . ."

"Oh, no," said Mrs. Camden.

"Tom Devlin had a family emergency, and I'm afraid we're going to have to fill in for him."

"But what about the birthday trip to my dad's?" Mrs. Camden asked. "The kids are looking forward to seeing their grandfather. And he's told me how much he's been looking forward to it, too."

"I'm sorry. We can reschedule the trip. Ask them if we can come out next week."

Mrs. Camden shook her head. "Next weekend and many of the weekends after that, Lucy will be checking out schools for next fall. And Mary will be heading back to Buffalo. Don't you remember? Your father already bought her the plane ticket. For Mary and Lucy, it's now or never."

The reverend nodded. He had known this would be an unwanted kink in the family's much-needed vacation plans, but he hadn't considered Mary's and Lucy's situations.

Reverend Camden sighed. "I don't know what I can do," he said. "You and I have got to go to this seminar—it's the most important gathering of the year. And you know I owe Tom Devlin a big favor. He filled in for me when I had my heart attack. Then when I was out with a cold— twice."

"I know, I know," Mrs. Camden replied, biting her lip.

"And it would be nice if we brought *some* of our children, seeing as how the conference is all about church *and* family."

Mrs. Camden shook her head sadly. "But the memory album was such a wonderful idea for a birthday gift—a way to help Dad remember us as he struggles with his Alzheimer's. We could send it, but it just doesn't feel right. Someone should be there. It's his birthday, after all."

She faced her husband. "And Lucy and Mary worked so hard to put all those pictures together. They'll be so disappointed if they can't give it to him in person."

Reverend Camden shrugged. "What are the choices?" he asked.

Suddenly a light went on in Mrs. Camden's head. "You know—"

"Don't say it," Reverend Camden warned.

"Hear me out," Mrs. Camden insisted.

"Mary's been out of high school for a year now. . . ."

Reverend Camden was already shaking his head.

"And Lucy is starting college in a few months," Mrs. Camden continued. "They aren't exactly children anymore."

"But Charles and Ginger live hundreds of miles away. Please tell me you're *not* saying we should let them drive to Phoenix alone?"

Before Mrs. Camden could reply, an excited voice cried, "Wow! Yeah, let us!"

They spun around to see Lucy and Mary standing in the kitchen. It was clear the girls had heard the last part of the discussion.

Mary and Lucy whooped and high-fived one another. Then they danced around the kitchen table, chanting, "Road trip! Road trip!"

Simon and Ruthie entered and stared at their older sisters.

"Hold on!" their father cried. "Nobody's going anywhere . . . at least, not without adult supervision. You two girls are not old enough to take a road trip. Not yet—not *ever,* if I have any say in the matter."

"But—"

Mrs. Camden crossed her arms, silencing her daughters for a moment. "The subject is under discussion between your father and me," she said. "This is a serious matter, and no decision has yet been made."

"But, Mom!" Lucy cried.

Mary edged her younger sister aside.

"Look, Mom, Dad," she began. "We're sorry for listening in on your private conversation, but Lucy and I both heard what you said about not going to Grandpa's this weekend—"

"Yeah," Lucy added. "And we think it stinks! We worked hard on Grandpa Charles's memory album, and we want to give it to him. In person. And on his birthday!"

"Not only that," Mary added. "I *am* an adult, remember?"

Reverend Camden shook his head. "I'm sorry," he said. "But I don't think it's a good idea to let you two girls go off to Arizona on your own."

Just then the telephone rang. As the discussion between father and daughters continued, Mrs. Camden picked up the phone.

"It's Dad," Mrs. Camden said a moment later. Everyone stopped talking.

"Dad says he can't wait to see his memory album. He and Ginger are asking what time we're going to arrive on Wednesday. It seems they can't wait to see us."

Reverend Camden looked confused. "Wednesday? But we're supposed to arrive on Friday."

Mrs. Camden nodded, her face sad. "His memory's deteriorating so quickly," she said softly.

Reverend Camden's shoulders sank.

Lucy and Mary gave their parents a look that said, *See, I told you so*.

Mrs. Camden pushed the receiver into her husband's hand.

"You'll break his heart," she said.

Reverend Camden handled the phone like it was a hot potato. He reluctantly put the receiver to his ear.

"Hi, Charles," he began. "Look, I'm really sorry, but something has come up this weekend . . . something to do with the church. Annie and I can't make it. But we promise we will come up in two weeks with Simon and Ruthie."

He paused, weighing his words.

"But Mary and Lucy *will* be driving up this weekend to deliver the memory album."

Mary and Lucy jumped up and down and screamed silently. Mrs. Camden frowned and shook her head.

"Yes, Charles, they *are* coming this weekend. . . . Yes, all by themselves. And they're both really looking forward to seeing you."

TWO

Reverend Camden hung up the phone, frowning.

Mrs. Camden reached out and touched his hand. "If it will make you feel any better, maybe Matt can go with them. Maybe if we talk to him, Matt *will* go with them. It doesn't hurt to ask."

Mary and Lucy were already gone. They had rushed up to their room to pack the moment they heard their father agree to their trip.

"I thought Matt had plans or something," Reverend Camden replied. "Isn't that why he's not visiting Grandpa Charles in the first place?"

"Did I just hear my name?" Matt said.

He came through the back door with a sack of dirty laundry in his arms.

"Matt!" Reverend Camden cried, patting his son's back. "It's good to see you."

Matt froze, instantly suspicious. He looked at his mother. She smiled innocently—too innocently, Matt thought.

"Something is definitely up," he said.

"How would you like to take a road trip this weekend?" Mrs. Camden asked, still smiling.

"I *am* taking a road trip this weekend, remember?" Matt said. "I'm going to Mountain View with John Hamilton and some other guys from school."

"But—"

"It's my *only* vacation, Dad. And it's practically free, which is always a plus. John even managed to score some tickets to the Mountain Music Festival on Saturday night."

"Sounds like fun," Reverend Camden admitted.

"But not more important than your sisters," Mrs. Camden said. "They're driving to Grandpa Charles's."

"Let's not get carried away, Mom. I'm

sure Mary and Lucy can handle the trip."

Ruthie came in and poured herself a glass of milk. Matt ruffled her hair when she sat down at the table and listened to the conversation.

"We really need you for this, Matt," Reverend Camden said. "Can't you help at all?"

"And *miss* my mountain getaway? A getaway I have been planning for weeks?" Matt shook his head. "I doubt it."

"What's a getaway?" Ruthie asked. "Did you rob a bank?"

Matt blinked.

Ruthie giggled. "Get it? Getaway. It's a pun."

"Very clever," Matt said, resisting a smile. "But for my purposes, it's a vacation."

Then he looked at his father. "The kind you can't pass up."

"Oh, Matt," Mrs. Camden sighed.

Matt raised his hand. "Don't panic, Mom. I think I've got this figured out."

"Then you'll go," Reverend Camden said hopefully.

"No," Matt replied. "But I think I can

find someone to watch out for them. Even if Mary and Lucy are all by themselves."

"But they are going to Arizona," Mrs. Camden said. "A whole other state! Mary and Lucy need someone there to watch out for them."

"Not if they watch out for each other," Matt replied.

Reverend Camden blinked. "I don't get it."

"I learned all about this in psychology class," Matt whispered conspiratorially. "I'll have a talk with Mary and Lucy, but *privately*. I'll tell each of them to watch out for the other one."

Mrs. Camden cocked her head. "I don't get it, either."

"It's simple. If Mary is watching Lucy, and Lucy is watching Mary, who has any time to get into trouble?"

Mrs. Camden looked doubtful.

"Trust me," Matt told her. "My plan will work."

"That's all well and good, son," his father said. "But I would love it if you did something *real* to help out in this situation."

"Real?" Matt replied. "Like what?"

Mrs. Camden stepped in, calming her overprotective husband. "Give the girls driving tips, safety instructions, directions, stuff like that," she said.

Matt smiled. "No problem, Mom. Consider it done. After all, you *are* talking to *the* most responsible driver in this family."

Later on, as Matt was pulling his clothes out of the washing machine, Mary came into the laundry room.

"I heard about your trip to Phoenix," Matt said, smiling.

Mary put her hands on her hips. "I suppose you're going to say that Lucy and I are too young and immature to make this trip alone."

"No," Matt replied. "I was going to say that I thought Lucy is too young and immature to make this trip, and I'm glad you are going to be with her."

Mary's jaw dropped. "Really?"

"Yep," Matt said, still smiling. "I think Lucy is in good hands. I'm going to give you both a list of things to check on the minivan, and I want you and Lucy to handle this stuff on your own so you know it's done right."

Matt reached out and patted Mary's hand. "I know at least *one* of you is mature enough to take care of things."

"Wow, Matt. You really . . . *surprised* me."

"I trust you," Matt said sincerely. "What's so surprising about that?"

Mary smiled proudly.

"And . . . just between you and me," Matt added in a whisper, "I trust you to look after Lucy, too. She needs you. Don't let her do anything stupid."

Mary threw her arms around her brother and hugged him.

"Thanks, Matt," she said. "Those were the nicest words you've said to me lately."

"Here's your clothes," Matt replied, handing Mary the stuff he had pulled out of the dryer and folded. "Now get upstairs and get ready for your trip. . . ."

Matt leaned close to Mary's ear. "And don't mention our little conversation to Lucy, okay?"

Mary gave him the thumbs-up sign, took her clothes, and went back to her room.

Fifteen minutes later, as Matt pulled his

work shirts out of the dryer, Lucy came in with an armful of dirty clothes.

"Washing stuff for your trip?" Matt asked.

Lucy nodded as she dumped the laundry into the washer and added detergent.

"Pretty exciting, huh?" Matt continued.

Lucy closed the lid on the washer, crossed her arms, and faced her brother.

"I guess you don't think this trip is a very good idea, do you, Matt?"

"No," he replied. "I think it's a *great* idea. It will be a real learning experience for Mary. I'm just glad you will be going along to watch out for her."

Lucy considered his words. Ever since Mary had gotten into legal and financial trouble, nobody trusted her. Even so, Lucy would always be looked upon as Mary's little sister. "And what about me?" she asked.

Matt smiled. "You're already covered."

Lucy cocked her head.

"What I mean to say is that I'm glad you will be there to take care of Mary. I know Mary is older than you, but you are the responsible one. Mary can be . . . well, *Mary.*"

Matt gave her a sincere look. "I trust you to keep her in line and not fall for any of her risky schemes."

Lucy smiled brightly. "You really trust me? Really?"

"Completely."

Then Matt leaned close to Lucy and whispered in her ear. "Just don't mention this conversation to Mary. You know how she gets."

Lucy winked. "My lips are sealed."

"Remember," he said. "I'm counting on you to be the brains on this trip."

Lucy nodded, smiling smugly.

Matt gathered up his clean clothes and stuffed them into a sack. Then he threw the bag over his shoulders and headed out to the car.

Beautifully acted, if I do say so myself, Matt thought. *Now both of them will be working so hard watching the other one that they won't have time to get into trouble.*

And, best of all, neither Mary nor Lucy realizes that I've been playing them like a piano. There really is something to this psychology stuff. . . .

Matt threw the sack in the backseat and climbed behind the wheel of his Camaro. He could almost taste the cool mountain air as visions of waterskiing, swimming, and fun filled his head.

THREE

"But I don't want to go to a dumb old family seminar! Seminars are for adults—and I'm barely a tween. Get it? I'm be*tween* a child and a teenager," Ruthie declared.

She was sitting in Simon's room, leafing through one of his martial arts magazines.

"Why not go to the seminar?" Simon replied. "Lots of other kids will be there. It might be fun."

"Mary and Lucy are having a safety seminar with Matt. Why can't I go to *that* one?"

Simon cackled. "A *safety* seminar— for the Destructor Twins? Like *that's* going to help. Mom and Dad are making a big mistake letting those two loose on the road."

"I'd still rather visit Grandpa and Ginger with Mary and Lucy," Ruthie said with a sigh.

Simon shook his head. "Believe me, you're better off sticking with Mom and Dad."

"Why?"

"Because Mary and Lucy will be all alone. Out there, in the big bad world. And they are totally unprepared for the experience. No safety seminar is going to change *that*."

Ruthie shrugged. "What could happen?"

"Plenty," Simon said ominously.

Mary was sitting at her desk, making a list of things she had to get done before the trip, when there was a knock on her door.

Mrs. Camden peeked through the door. "Mary, can I talk to you?"

"Sure, Mom, come in."

Mrs. Camden handed Mary a Radio Shack bag.

"I bought this for you. . . . You and Lucy, that is."

Mary pulled out a cell phone, a battery pack, a battery charger, and an adapter.

"Wow, thanks!"

"It's for your trip," Mrs. Camden explained. "And I want to tell you something."

Sensing her mother's serious mood, Mary set aside her work.

"When I was your age, I went on a similar trip," Mrs. Camden began. "I still remember it as one of the best times of my life. But it's a big responsibility we're giving you. I want you to promise me that you'll have this phone on at all times and that you will call in regularly."

Mary smiled. "Don't worry, Mom. We'll be fine."

Mrs. Camden nodded, wanting to believe her daughter. She knew her motherly fears were normal, but that didn't make them any less troublesome. She also knew that Phoenix was only a day away and that her daughters were both resourceful and responsible.

She looked at Mary again. "The point is, this phone—and the reassuring sound of your voice speaking to me on a regular basis—will keep your mother from worrying. So use it. Please."

"Sure, Mom," Mary said, nodding. "And try not to worry so much, okay?"

"That's my job," Mrs. Camden replied. "You'll find out yourself when you have children of your own."

"Which, hopefully, will be a long time in the future. I want to have fun first."

Mrs. Camden shook her head. "How reassuring."

Lucy was surprised to find Matt knocking on her door.

"I thought you went home," she said.

"I'm back," Matt replied. He handed her a piece of paper.

"What's this?"

"It's the maintenance list I promised you," Matt explained. "I went back to my apartment and wrote it up."

Lucy scanned the list. It was pretty thorough and included checks on the oil, the spare tire, brake and transmission fluids, windshield wiper fluid, the radiator. . . .

"Spark plugs?" Lucy cried. "Why should I check the spark plugs?"

"If they get dirty, they don't spark

right," Matt explained. "You waste gas."

Lucy thrust the list back at Matt.

"I don't need this," she said. "I know more about fixing cars than *you* do."

"That's true." Matt pushed the list back at her. "But I have been driving a lot longer than you have. I know the kinds of things that can go wrong."

Lucy looked at the list again.

"Pretend you're an airplane pilot," Matt said. "They have checklists they have to follow before they take off. If you just follow this checklist, everything should go fine."

Lucy thought about it for a minute.

"Do it for me," Matt said sincerely. "Do it because I gave the list to *you*. And do you know why? Because *you* are the responsible one."

"Okay," she replied, finally nodding. "I'll follow the list. But only because you have faith in me."

"Thanks. And just in case you forget this checklist, I've taped a copy of it on the dashboard of the minivan."

"Don't worry," Lucy said, her tone smug. "We responsible types don't forget important things."

"That's the spirit!" Matt replied, patting

her back. "Now go find Mary."

Lucy arched her eyebrow. "Why?"

"Because it's time for your safety seminar," said Matt.

Lucy held up the paper. "But I've got the list."

"This lecture is going to be a little different," Matt told her. "And I promised Mom and Dad I would give you both a talk. So meet me in the kitchen in five minutes."

"Yes, sir!" Lucy said with a salute.

In the hallway, Ruthie heard the end of the conversation and her ears perked up. She scampered down the stairs and ran into the kitchen before anyone else saw her.

Six minutes later, Lucy and Mary sat at the kitchen table, waiting for Matt to begin.

"First of all, here's a map," Matt said, handing it to Mary.

"We already *have* maps," she replied.

Matt snorted. "Of the right state? The last time you followed a map, it was a map of Florida, and we were in California. Do you remember?"

Mary blushed. "Point taken."

"Okay, listen up," Matt continued. "Here are the rules of the road."

"Another list?" Mary said, sharing a look with Lucy.

"No," said Matt, "just three basic rules." He held up his index finger.

"One, do *not* take an unprepared car on a long road trip. I've given Lucy a maintenance list, and I suggest you both stick to it."

The girls nodded.

"Two," Matt said, "do *not* talk to strangers. I don't care how cute they are, or if they look like they need help. Do not talk to strangers. Period."

"Duh," Lucy grunted. "I learned that in kindergarten."

"And three," Matt continued, "do *not*, under any circumstances, pick up a hitchhiker."

"Like we would *ever* do that," Mary snorted.

"What if you're driving on a lonely country road at night and you see a young, innocent girl walking along the side of the road? Would you pick her up?"

Matt stared at them.

"Well," Lucy said, "I might try to help her. . . ."

"No!" Matt cried.

"Huh?"

"I'm going to tell you a story about what happened to one of John Hamilton's friends when he picked up a hitchhiker."

"Do tell," Mary giggled.

"He was driving alone late at night when he saw a young girl walking along a deserted stretch of highway. Worried that something might happen to her, he stopped the car—"

"—to ask for a date?" Mary quipped. "Sounds like one of *John's* friends."

Matt shushed her. "The girl didn't talk much," he continued. "But she did tell him that her home was a few miles up the road, so he offered the girl a ride."

Matt lowered his voice ominously. "It was a ride that changed his life forever. . . ."

"Wha—what happened?" Lucy asked, eyes wide.

"When they stopped in front of her house a few minutes later—the girl was gone!"

"Gone?"

"She vanished from the seat right next to him. One minute she was there. The next—poof!"

"Poof? What did he do?" Lucy asked.

"He knocked at the door of the house. After a long time, an old woman answered. John's friend apologized for waking her and told the woman he just wanted to make sure her daughter got into the house okay."

Mary just rolled her eyes.

"Suddenly," Matt continued, "the old woman began to cry. . . ."

Lucy frowned.

"Then the old woman told him that her daughter was—"

"—dead!" Mary cried, jumping to her feet. "Killed in a hit-and-run accident on that very stretch of road. The hitchhiker John's friend picked up was a ghost!"

By the expression on Matt's face, Lucy could tell Mary had guessed the ending.

"How did you know?" Lucy asked her sister.

"Because I heard the very same *lame* story at summer camp when I was nine,"

Mary replied. Then she looked at her brother.

"I can't believe you'd try to scare us with a stupid old ghost story. We're not kids, you know."

"Yeah," Lucy added. "That story *was* pretty lame."

"But it had you going," he said. "Admit it."

"I don't think that story would scare Ruthie," Mary said with a shake of her head.

"Oh, I don't know. I'm pretty scared," whispered a timid voice.

Matt lifted the tablecloth.

Ruthie was cowering there. Her eyes were wide. She was almost as pale as a ghost herself.

"What are you doing down there?" Matt teased.

"I just wanted to hear the safety seminar," Ruthie replied, jumping into her big brother's arms.

"Well, well," Mary said. "Little Miss Big Pants isn't so big anymore!"

FOUR

It was a busy Friday morning at the Camden house. Mary and Lucy were loading the minivan for their trip. Mrs. Camden was trying to get the twins ready for the drive across town to the seminar. Simon and Ruthie were dressing and bickering at the same time.

Outside, in the driveway, Lucy was running down the checklist Matt had given her. She had a pencil in her hand and she made a mark beside each item.

"Oil . . . check. Wiper fluid . . . check. First-aid kit . . . check."

"Will you can it?" Mary cried, dropping her suitcase. "I've already taken the time to go over the car. Let's get this show on the road."

Lucy tapped the list with her pencil. "It would have been nice if you helped me prep the car yesterday. But you had better things to do. Now you'll just have to be patient while I go over this list— carefully."

"Oh, so you're the responsible one because you never get into trouble? Well, I'm older. I've been out in the world."

Lucy returned to the checklist, smiling inwardly. *Of course I'm the responsible one—Matt said so himself.*

"Brake fluid . . . that's a check. . . . Transmission fluid . . . check. . . ."

Reverend Camden came outside and watched his daughters for a moment. It looked like Matt's psychological experiment had failed. Mary and Lucy were bickering, and they hadn't even left the driveway yet.

"All ready?" he asked the girls.

Mary made a face. "We're packed, but we're not going anywhere. Lucy'll be checking that list of hers until Monday morning."

"Don't give me false hope," Reverend Camden sighed.

Mary and Lucy both rolled their eyes.

"Anyway," Reverend Camden continued, "I just came out to wish you both well. And I think it's good that Lucy's so—"

Mary's eyes narrowed. "Annoying?"

"—thorough."

"Thanks, Dad," Lucy said, shooting a look at her sister.

"Anyway," he said, "I'm here to say goodbye and to give you this."

Reverend Camden handed Mary a plastic card. Her eyes went wide.

"A—a credit card?" she stammered, surprised that he'd give her a card after she'd had so many credit card problems in the past.

"It's for emergencies," he added quickly. "Just in case the minivan breaks down, or you're stuck and need a place to stay, or . . ."

Mary and Lucy both hugged him.

"Thanks, Dad," Lucy said.

"You're the best," said Mary.

"You're welcome." He smiled and embraced them both tightly.

"And don't worry," Mary added, "we won't abuse the credit card."

"Well," Reverend Camden said, "don't restrain yourselves *too* much. I mean, you can certainly buy something . . . for yourselves. Within reason, that is. . . ."

He paused, regarding his daughters. Then he reached into his pocket. "And here's some cash for anyplace that won't take plastic."

He handed Mary the money. Then he took a long look at his daughters.

"I have to get back inside," he said at last. "Your mother needs help getting the twins ready for the seminar. I'll say good-bye later."

When he was gone, Mary looked at Lucy.

"Remember that fancy mall near Grandpa Charles's house? I wonder how good the shops really are?"

They both began to giggle.

Matt rolled over and moaned when the alarm clock sounded. He had been up too late the night before, packing for his trip. He couldn't believe it was time to get up already.

He reached out and switched off the alarm.

Matt wanted to see Mary and Lucy off. And he still had to get his car checked out before he left for the mountains. But it was so hard to get out of bed. . . .

"Just five more minutes," he muttered to himself as his eyes closed. A moment later, Matt was snoring loudly.

The Camdens were about ready to leave for the seminar. The electric van was charged, and Simon and Ruthie sat with the twins in the back.

Mrs. Camden glanced at her watch. "I thought Matt was coming by to see everybody off," she said.

"You mean to check up on Mary and Lucy," Reverend Camden replied. "Don't worry, Matt's probably at the gas station getting his Camaro checked out for his trip to the mountains."

They stood together next to the electric van, watching as Mary and Lucy threw the last of their stuff into the other minivan.

"It looks like they're almost ready to go," Reverend Camden said.

Mrs. Camden took his hand in hers.

"Don't worry. They're good kids. They'll be fine. . . ."

"I hope so," Reverend Camden sighed.

So do I, Mrs. Camden thought.

"Hey, I almost forgot!" Simon cried, jumping out of the electric car and running over to his sisters. "I have something for your trip."

"Not another list, I hope," said Mary.

Simon thrust an aerosol can into her hand. Mary glanced at it.

"Mace?" she cried. "You're giving us a can of Mace?"

Simon shrugged. "It's a big bad world out there. You never know. . . ."

Mary handed the Mace to Lucy, who stuck it in her purse.

It was time to go. Mary and Lucy stood with their parents. No one knew quite what to say. Finally, Mary broke the spell.

"Well, I guess this is goodbye," she said.

Everyone hugged, then headed for their vehicles. A moment later, Mrs. Camden sat in the electric car next to her husband. They both watched as Mary and Lucy drove away.

"Come on, Mom," Simon said. "They'll

be okay. It's not like we're sending them off to their doom or something."

Reaching over his mother's shoulder, Simon switched on the radio. The love theme from *Titanic* filled the van.

Reverend Camden saw the expression on his wife's face and quickly turned the radio off.

"Maybe this isn't the right time for music," he said.

Two hours later, Matt was racing his Camaro toward the outskirts of Glenoak. Traffic was already heavy, and he was nowhere near the highway that would take him to Mountain View.

"So much for an early start," he muttered to himself.

When he'd turned off the alarm, Matt thought he was just going to close his eyes for another five minutes. Instead he woke up almost two hours later.

He threw on his clothes, tossed his luggage into the trunk, and got on the road. It was too late to see Mary and Lucy off. Too late to do any of the other things he wanted to get done, including having his car checked.

"Well, I had the oil changed last month," he reasoned. "Or was it the month before?"

Then Matt patted the dashboard.

"It doesn't matter, right?" he said. "You won't let me down, will you?"

Less than a minute later, gray smoke began to pour out from under Matt's hood. On the dashboard, the oil light was blinking red.

"Oh, no," Matt cried. He peered into the rearview mirror. He was leaving a trail of smoke.

As Matt steered his car into a nearby gas station, the smoke turned from gray to black.

A gas station attendant ran over to the car.

"Cut your engine, kid!" the man called. "It looks like you've blown a gasket."

Matt climbed out of the car and together they peered under the hood. The repairman tinkered with the engine for a few minutes.

"It's not that bad, after all," the mechanic said finally.

Matt sighed with relief. "How long will it take to fix?"

The man shrugged. "An hour or two, once I get the parts. You can have her back by Monday afternoon."

"Monday!" Matt cried. "But I need it *today*."

"Then you should have taken better care of it. There's almost no oil in this baby, and the pump is shot."

"Isn't there something you can do?"

The man shook his head. "I'll order the parts right now. But it's Friday, which means I won't have it until Monday morning."

"But I was going on a trip," Matt whined.

"Sorry, son," the man replied. "You're not going anywhere. Not in this car, anyway."

FIVE

"It's my turn to drive," Mary said as she fanned herself with the map.

Lucy pulled down her sunglasses and glanced at the clock on the dashboard.

"We're not even out of California. I've only been driving for two hours," she said. "I know because I set the clock this morning—as you can see, I checked that item off on the safety list."

"The safety list! The safety list!" Mary cried. "When are you going to give it a rest?"

The heady freedom of the road had worn off after the first hour. Then the sisters had begun a sing-along session. But after an hour of that, boredom set in. Mary got restless and began to bug Lucy about driving.

"We'll never get to Grandpa Charles's at this rate. You're barely driving at the speed limit."

"There's a *range* of speed limits," Lucy replied. "The limit is sixty-five, the minimum speed is forty-five—"

"And we're going about forty!" Mary complained. "You drive slower than the school librarian—"

"Mrs. Sneerson isn't slow. She's just cautious," Lucy countered.

"She's slow!" Mary insisted. "And so are you." Then she pointed to a sign. "There's a rest stop. Pull over and let me take the wheel."

Lucy left the highway and drove up the ramp that led to the rest stop. She parked across the lot from the only other vehicle, a battered pickup truck covered with dust and grime.

The rest area looked like a small park. It had trees and grass, picnic tables, and a comfort station.

"I'm going to the ladies' room," Lucy said.

Mary nudged her sister. "Do you see that?" she asked.

Lucy blinked. "It's kind of hard not to."

They had both spotted a girl, about their own age, near the picnic tables. It looked as if she was searching through the garbage cans. The girl was hard to miss, because she wore blue jeans and a bright orange vest. Her hair was also colored bright orange. She looked a little like a walking safety cone.

"What do you think she's doing?" Mary asked.

Lucy shrugged. "Maybe she lost something."

Trying not to stare, the girls headed off to the rest room.

A few minutes later, they emerged into the bright late-morning sunshine.

"Oh, no!" Lucy grabbed her sister's arm.

Two men in scruffy clothes were beside their vehicle. One had a coat hanger. He was thrusting it through a crack in the window, trying to release the lock.

"They're trying to break into our minivan. What . . . what do we do?" Mary whispered.

Lucy reached into her purse. "I've got the Mace."

But Mary shook her head. "Maybe we should just call the police. Let them handle it."

"Give me the cell phone."

"I left it in the van!"

Lucy frowned. "There's a pay phone over there. But those guys will see us if we try to call anybody."

Mary's eyes narrowed. "I'm getting mad now. They have no right—"

She was interrupted by a loud shriek. They turned to see the girl in the orange vest rushing the two guys. She had a thick branch in her hands. She swung it like a club.

"We better help!" Mary cried, running forward.

"No!" Lucy said. But Mary was already running toward the commotion. Lucy held the can of Mace in front of her and followed.

The girl in the orange vest was swinging the stick wildly, and it connected with one guy's head.

He howled and took off. The other

man raised his fist, then saw Mary and Lucy coming for him.

He took off, too.

The men jumped into the battered pickup truck and, seconds later, sped away.

The girl in the vest dropped her stick and plopped down on the pavement, trembling. Mary and Lucy rushed to her side.

"Are you all right?" Lucy asked.

"That was really something," said Mary.

The girl looked up at them. Her face was dirty, and so were her clothes. Her orange hair was messed up, and there were leaves stuck in it, like she had been lying on the ground.

She looked up at them. "Is this your car?" she asked.

"Yes." Lucy nodded. "Thank you for chasing those guys away."

The girl shrugged. "I saw those creeps come in about a half hour ago. I knew they were looking for trouble, so I hid over by the garbage cans."

"Well, you sure knew how to handle them," Mary said with admiration. "My name is Mary . . . Mary Camden. And this is my sister Lucy."

The girl got to her feet and dusted off her jeans.

"My name is Sandi," she said, thrusting out her dirty hand. Mary and Lucy both shook it.

Sandi looked down at her ragged, filthy clothes, then back at the nicely dressed Camden girls.

"You don't happen to have something to eat, do you?" she asked. "Anything at all would be fine. . . ."

Lucy blinked. She scanned the parking lot. There were no other vehicles.

"Are you stuck here?" Lucy asked.

Sandi nodded. "I got a ride late last night. But the truck driver was getting off at the next exit, so he left me here. I've been trying to find a ride all morning. Not to mention something to eat."

Mary and Lucy exchanged glances.

"Hey," Sandi said, "could you give me a lift? Maybe just to the next rest stop. I'd really appreciate it."

Lucy frowned but said nothing.

Mary thought about it. Normally, she

wouldn't have hesitated, but she remembered what Matt had said. *She* was the responsible one. Which meant she was capable of making the right decision. And this girl was clearly harmless and in need.

"Sure," Mary said at last. "We'll get you some food. But first, let's get you cleaned up. I'm sure I have something in my suitcase that will fit you."

Sandi smiled her thanks.

"That's some jacket," Mary added.

Sandi laughed and fingered the orange vest. "I was cold yesterday—or maybe it was the day before. Anyway, this guy at a construction site gave it to me. Or maybe that was three days ago. . . ."

Mary climbed into the minivan and opened her suitcase. Lucy climbed in next to her sister and poked Mary in the ribs.

"What are you doing?" she whispered.

"We can't just leave Sandi here," Mary replied. "And keep it down or she'll hear you."

"Don't you remember what Matt said?"

Mary waved her sister away. "Don't worry. Her name is Sandi. And I'm absolutely certain that she's not a ghost."

"But—"

"Anyway, she helped us. The least we can do is help her."

Mary pulled a sweatshirt and a pair of shorts out of her luggage and handed them to Sandi.

"Let's get you cleaned up," Mary said, leading Sandi to the comfort station.

Lucy sighed and leaned against the minivan.

"Three lousy rules, and she breaks them all," she muttered. "Matt was right when he said *I'm* the responsible one. I'll bet Matt would never talk to a stranger."

_____

SIX

"Bus number sixty-five to Joshua Tree, Rabbit Hollow, Los Pinos, and Michaels Canyon, with connections to Quail Run and Mountain View, is now arriving at gate six. . . ."

Matt stood up and stretched when he heard the announcement, then grabbed his backpack and headed for the gate.

He checked his watch and smiled. The bus was right on time.

When his Camaro had broken down, Matt was sure his vacation was ruined. Then he remembered that John Hamilton had gone to Mountain View by bus just yesterday.

Maybe there was a bus *every* day!

Matt had rushed across town to the bus station and had arrived barely half an hour before the last bus was scheduled to depart.

Though he used most of his cash to buy the ticket, Matt wasn't worried. Once he got to Mountain View, his room and board were free, so he didn't need money, anyway. And he knew he could always bum a ride back to Glenoak from someone.

Matt was proud of his own resourcefulness. He'd made the bus and got the tickets. Now he could relax. Sure, he would arrive a little later than planned, but there would still be plenty of time to have fun.

There were lots of people waiting at the gate when Matt arrived. He immediately noted a pretty young woman in the crowd. She had shoulder-length blond hair and bright blue eyes.

Matt didn't want to stare, but he couldn't help it.

Suddenly their eyes met and she smiled.

The doors on the bus swung open, and people began to board. The driver checked Matt's ticket.

"You'll be transferring to another bus in Michaels Canyon," he said.

"I know," Matt said. "Will we make it on time?"

"No sweat. The other bus always waits for us."

Matt moved through the crowded aisle. Most of the seats were already taken.

"You can sit here," a sweet voice said.

Matt turned and saw the pretty blonde. She was patting the seat next to her.

Matt smiled. *This is my lucky day*.

"My name is Terry," the girl said, offering Matt her hand.

"Hi," Matt said, smiling, "I'm Matt. Matthew Camden. Pleased to meet you."

He stuffed his backpack into the jammed rack above his seat. Then he sat down.

"So," Terry began, "where are you headed?"

"I'm going to Mountain View."

"Nice place. Do you live there?"

"Nah," Matt said. "I'm just going for a weekend getaway."

"Lucky you," Terry said with a chuckle. "I'm only going as far as Rabbit Hollow."

In a cloud of fumes, the bus left the

station. Minutes later, it was rolling down the highway.

"Do you go to school?" Matt asked. "College, I mean."

"Heavens, no," Terry replied. "I graduated a long time ago. But thanks for the compliment."

Terry broke out some cheese and crackers, which she shared with Matt. While they ate, they talked.

"So you live in Glenoak," Terry said. "Do you live at home?"

"No way," Matt said. "I'm too old to live with my family. I have an off-campus apartment that I share with a friend. But I do have a family."

Matt pulled out his wallet and showed Terry some photos. "I have three sisters and three brothers. But I'm the oldest, and the first one out of the house."

"That's a big family. Sounds like fun."

Matt stuffed his wallet into his shirt pocket, next to his bus ticket.

"So," Terry asked, "what are you studying in college?"

"Premed," Matt said proudly. "I want to be a doctor."

"Wow," Terry said, impressed.

"It's tough, but I want to make medi-cine my life."

"Good luck," she replied.

"What do you do?"

Terry sighed. "Right now, I'm between jobs. I'm not sure what I want to do next, not that I have many options. I suppose I might go back to Las Vegas. Back to my old job. If I can find the money to get back there."

It was Matt's turn to be impressed.

"I've never been to Las Vegas," he said. "Is the town as wild as they say it is?"

"Oh, no. It's much wilder."

Matt wanted to know more, but Terry quickly changed the subject.

"I think this part of the country is beautiful. And Mountain View is a lovely place. Are you going to the lake?"

Matt told her about his plans and his friends. But as the bus rolled along, the landscape blurring as it flashed by and the vibration of the engine made Matt sleepy.

"Sorry," Matt said, stifling a yawn. "I was up late last night. Too late."

"Go ahead and take a nap," Terry said, opening a magazine. "I'll wake you up before I get off. Just to say goodbye."

"Thanks." Matt sat back in the seat and closed his eyes. A moment later, he was fast asleep.

"Wake up, kid," a loud voice said into Matt's ear. "It's the end of the line."

Matt sat up, rubbing his eyes.

"Come on," the bus driver barked. "You'll miss your connection."

"Wha . . . where's Terry?"

"Who?"

"The girl who was sitting next to me," Matt said. "She was going to wake me up when we got to Rabbit Hollow."

"Well, that was an hour ago. I guess she forgot."

Matt thanked the man and snatched his backpack from the rack. As he left the bus, he fumbled for the other ticket in his shirt pocket.

It was gone. So was his wallet. *And* the little bit of money he had left.

Matt ran back to the bus and pounded on the door.

"I lost my ticket!" Matt cried. "And my wallet!"

The driver let Matt search around his seat. But the ticket and wallet were gone.

"Where could they be?" Matt wondered.

The bus driver shook his head. "Off the top of my head, I'd say that the girl you were sitting with robbed you."

"Huh?"

"I've seen it before," said the driver. "Somebody falls asleep, and the passenger next to him steals his wallet, his luggage, or his ticket."

"What good would a ticket be?" Matt said. "Unless she wanted to go to Mountain View?"

"She can always cash it in for a refund," the man said with a shrug.

In shock, Matt stumbled off the bus. Without money *or* a bus ticket, he was stranded.

What am I going to do?

Matt glumly watched as the bus for Mountain View drove away, leaving him in the dust.

SEVEN

Mary and Lucy watched in amazement as Sandi took a huge bite out of her third cheeseburger. She barely chewed the mouthful before she swallowed it. After a sip of Coke, she immediately took another bite.

"So," Lucy said above the noise in the fast-food restaurant, "can we help you with anything else? A telephone call to your folks, maybe? How about a bus ticket home? We have to get back on the road, so—"

Mary poked Lucy in the ribs.

"Take your time," Mary said, touching Sandi's arm. "We'll *all* get back on the road when you're finished eating."

Lucy shot Mary a look. Mary returned fire. Sandi nodded between gobbles.

Finally, Lucy folded her arms and sat back in her chair, fuming.

Fifteen minutes later, Sandi had finished eating and was returning from the rest room. Cleaned up and wearing Mary's clothes, Sandi looked like a normal teenage girl.

Well, a normal teenage girl with a pierced nose and orange hair, anyway.

But Lucy knew it was wrong to judge a book by its cover. And she couldn't help but wonder what had driven Sandi out into the world before she was ready.

Nobody should have to look for food in a garbage can, thought Lucy.

Of course, she was happy to buy Sandi a meal or even a bus ticket. It was the least she and Mary could do after Sandi had chased the thieves away from their minivan.

But Lucy wasn't at all happy that Mary had offered Sandi a ride all the way to Phoenix, just because the girl said she was thinking of moving to New York City.

"We're driving east, so we'll be going in the same direction as you, anyway. We might as well give you a ride," Mary had insisted.

Lucy knew Mary was doing the right thing by helping Sandi. But she wasn't convinced that Mary was giving Sandi the proper kind of help.

A girl like Sandi was too young to be out on her own. She must have parents or something. People who missed her, who were worried about her. Helping this girl run away from whatever her problems were just didn't seem right, as far as Lucy was concerned.

Mary had tried to discover why Sandi was out on her own. When they had turned off the highway to find a restaurant, Mary had asked Sandi about her background. But the girl refused to talk about her life. She kept saying she wanted to go to New York, where "her best friend was waiting for her."

That was when Mary offered Sandi a ride to Phoenix—a move that made Lucy very angry. After the safety lecture from Matt, her sister should have known better!

Well, Lucy thought, *it's only a few hours. And I'll make sure to keep that can of Mace close by, where I can reach it!*

"All done?" Mary asked.

"Those burgers were great," Sandi said. "I can't thank you enough."

"Don't worry about it," Mary replied.

"Yeah," Lucy added less enthusiastically, "don't worry about it."

"Let's go," said Mary, jumping to her feet.

Sandi rose and grabbed the orange vest she'd draped over her chair. Even after Mary gave her clean clothes, Sandi refused to lose the vest the construction worker had given her.

"I like it," she told them. "It matches my hair."

Out in the parking lot, Mary and Lucy began to argue about the same old thing.

"It's my turn to drive," Mary cried.

"No way!" Lucy shot back. "You're going to take care of our . . . guest. I'll do the driving."

"Oh, no, you don't. . . ."

"Look," Lucy hissed under her breath, "you offered Sandi a ride—now you deal with her. I'm going to drive, and you're going to talk some sense into that girl."

"But it's my turn," Mary whispered back.

"Too bad, because I'm the one holding the keys," Lucy replied, dangling them in Mary's face.

As they drove out of the parking lot, Lucy became confused.

"When we left the highway, did we make a right turn or a left turn?" she asked.

"Right," Mary said instantly.

"I don't think so," Lucy said. "Now that I look at the road, I'm sure we turned left."

"Then why did you ask?" Mary shot back. "And you're wrong, anyway. We turned *right*!"

Lucy peered at the road. There were no signs, and neither way looked familiar. She groaned.

"Are you sure we turned right?"

"Yes," Mary said.

"No," Sandi added. "I think we turned left."

Lucy hit the steering wheel. "You can't *both* be right!" she cried.

"Look, we turned right," Mary insisted. "I'm sure of it. Just backtrack the way we came and you'll find the highway. Or give me the keys and I'll drive."

Sandi shrugged. "Whatever."

"Okay," Lucy said, turning right.

Fifteen minutes later, they found themselves driving along a lonely country road with no signs and almost no traffic.

"I knew we should have turned left!" Lucy cried. "I'm going to turn around."

"Wait until you see a gas station," Mary said. "We can pull in and ask for directions."

"But I haven't seen a gas station for ten miles."

Just then, the minivan's engine sputtered, then died. Momentum carried the car a few more yards as Lucy steered it to the shoulder of the road.

Finally the minivan rolled to a halt.

"What's wrong?" Mary asked.

"Nothing's wrong!" Lucy shot back. "I mean, I didn't do anything wrong. It must be the minivan."

Lucy turned the key, trying to restart the engine.

Nothing happened.

Then she saw the warning light blinking on the dashboard.

"Oh, no," Lucy moaned.

"I can't believe this," Mary complained.

"It's not my fault," Lucy cried. "I followed the checklist!"

Mary scanned Matt's list, which was still taped to the dashboard. "It's not on the list. . . ."

"It—it must be," Lucy stammered.

"Nope," Mary said, shaking her head. "Just about everything else is on that list. But not that."

"But how could we have forgotten something so . . . so basic?"

"We?" Mary shot back. *"You* were the one following Matt's checklist, remember. I just looked the van over."

"Then maybe you should have looked at the gas gauge!"

In the backseat, Sandi's eyes went wide. "You mean—"

"Yep," Mary said with a sigh, "we're out of gas."

Mary and Lucy exchanged glances. They climbed out of the minivan.

"Time to call Mom," Lucy declared.

"No way," Mary cried. "I'm not going to call now. They'll think we can't take care of ourselves."

Lucy threw up her hands. "Obviously, we *can't.* Now call."

"Fine," Mary said. She pulled the cell phone out of her purse and activated it.

Nothing happened.

"What now?" Lucy demanded.

"I . . . I think the batteries are dead," Mary said, blushing.

Lucy exploded.

"I can't believe this. I prepped the minivan. I ran the checklist. All *you* had to do was change the stupid batteries!"

"Don't panic," Mary replied. "I have a battery charger in my suitcase."

"Where are you going to plug it in?"

"The lighter," Mary said smugly.

Lucy snorted. "Then you need an adapter."

Mary frowned. "I hadn't thought of that."

"Obviously," said Lucy, folding her arms across her chest.

"Maybe we can—"

But Lucy hushed her. "Do you feel something?" she said softly.

Then Mary felt it, too. The ground beneath their feet seemed to vibrate, and they heard a noise—it sounded like an airplane taking off or the roar of a hundred engines.

And the noise was getting louder. And closer, too. So close it was rumbling in their chests.

"I don't like the sound of that," Lucy said, reaching for her can of Mace.

EIGHT

Michaels Canyon wasn't really a town. It was just a canyon dotted with pine trees that had a street running down the middle. The only signs of civilization were the street, the bus stop, and a boarded-up convenience store.

The convenience store looked like it had gone out of business a long time ago. And the tiny bus stop closed at one-thirty in the afternoon, shortly after the last bus for Mountain View departed.

The mountains were a blue line in the distance.

Stranded and penniless, Matt sat down on a bench and wondered what he was going to do next.

At any other time, he would have called his parents. Except that this time they weren't at home. His mom and dad had a cell phone, of course, for just such an emergency. But Matt had never had an emergency before and he couldn't remember the phone number.

He'd written it down on a piece of paper and had placed the note inside his wallet. The same wallet that had been stolen along with his money and bus ticket.

Suddenly, Matt's stomach rumbled. He was in such a hurry to get out of Glenoak that he had forgotten to eat anything.

He spotted a vending machine sitting against the outside wall of the bus station. Pretzels, potato chips, and cheese twists beckoned to him through the glass.

Matt counted the change in his pocket. He had just enough to cover a bag of pretzels.

He fed the machine and made his selection. But when he pressed the button, nothing happened. He pressed the coin return, but it didn't work, either.

Matt shook the machine, but it would

not let go of the pretzels, or his money.

Then he felt a presence. Someone was standing behind him. Matt turned to find a policeman watching from behind dark sunglasses.

"Got a problem, son?" the policeman asked.

Matt sighed with relief. He told the officer about the robbery, and about missing the bus to Mountain View, and about being stuck in Michaels Canyon.

The policeman listened quietly. When Matt was finished, the man sighed. "I was wondering what was going on," he said. "I got a call that a vagrant was hanging around the bus stop."

"Vagrant?" Matt cried. "I'm not a vagrant. I'm a college student!"

"You said you have no money, right?"

Matt nodded.

"And your identification was stolen, right?"

Matt nodded.

"Well, son, in this county, if you don't have ID or cash, you're a vagrant."

"What am I supposed to do?"

The policeman pointed to the end of

the street. "If you walk about five miles in that direction, you'll find the highway. I suggest you start walking now."

Matt was stunned. "But—"

"I'm going on patrol. If you're still here when I get back, I'll have no choice but to arrest you for vagrancy, and you'll spend thirty days in the county jail."

Then the policeman walked to his squad car.

"Oh," he said, turning back to Matt, "hitchhiking is illegal in this county, too, so don't try bumming a ride until you've walked at least three miles and crossed the county line."

"Yes, sir," Matt said. "I'll . . . I'll be on my way."

When the policeman drove off, Matt leaned against the vending machine. Suddenly he heard a mechanical click, and the bag of pretzels dropped into the slot.

Grabbing the bag, Matt turned his eyes skyward.

"Thank you," he whispered gratefully as he tore it open.

The roar of engines was so intense that it shook the road. Mary and Lucy watched as a dozen motorcycles, all shiny chrome and hot, roaring metal, streaked around the corner—heading right for them!

Sandi jumped out of the minivan and hopped up and down as the bikers approached.

"They're the bomb!" she cried, waving.

Lucy couldn't believe it. She was even more stunned when Mary nodded in agreement with Sandi.

"Really cool," Mary cried, watching the black-leather-clad drivers steer their powerful machines.

Lucy reached into her purse and grabbed the can of Mace. She saw the helmeted head of the lead driver turn in their direction. Her knees suddenly went weak.

"Here they come," she gasped.

The cycle in the lead pulled up next to the minivan and skidded to a halt. The driver, face invisible under the red helmet, gunned the engine once, then cut it.

The other motorcycles quickly surrounded them.

Like a trapped animal, Lucy backed up until her body was pressed against the minivan. Her white knuckles clutched the

Mace as her eyes rose in prayer.

The driver of the lead cycle, who was clad from neck to toe in black leather, stepped off the bike. Gloved hands reached up and pulled off the helmet.

Lucy gasped in surprise. Sandi whooped. And Mary smiled.

The cycle gang's leader shook her long red hair loose and brushed it back. "Looks like you're having a little trouble," she said brightly.

The other bikers cut their engines and pulled off their helmets, too.

"You—you're all girls," Lucy stammered.

The leader stuck out her hand. "Hi," she said, "I'm Maggie." Then she gestured to the other cyclists. "And these are Heaven's Angels."

"Are you real bikers?" Sandi asked.

"We're a stunt-driving act out of Los Angeles," Maggie replied. "We're heading up to Mountain View to drive in the big motor rally and see the music festival."

"I'm really pleased to meet you," Mary said, shaking the woman's hand. "And I love your bikes."

"Harleys," Maggie said proudly. "Made in the USA. They're the best."

"What's the problem?" another biker asked the girls. Her face was streaked with oil and her hair was spiked like Simon's used to be.

"We ran out of gas," Lucy said, hiding the Mace can behind her back.

Maggie shook her head. "Bad place to do it. You're miles from the highway."

"I know," Lucy said, shooting Mary a look. "We made a wrong turn."

As they spoke, a biker with a sidecar of supplies brought out a can of gas and a funnel. In seconds she was filling the minivan's tank.

"You won't get far on this," Maggie told them. "But it'll be enough gas to get you to the highway, where you can find a gas station."

"Where *is* the highway?" Mary asked.

Maggie gave them directions. Then the biker who filled their tank helped them get the minivan started. When the engine was purring, Maggie hopped back onto her motorcycle.

"Have a safe trip," she said with a wave.

"You too," Mary called. "And thanks for everything."

Then, in a cloud of dust, Heaven's Angels roared down the open road and vanished.

"My turn to drive," Mary said, snatching the keys out of Lucy's hand.

NINE

"This is the third time I've tried to call Mary and Lucy," Mrs. Camden told her husband.

They were in a large, crowded hall across town, where the two-day Family and Church Ministers Conference was in full swing.

"And?" asked Reverend Camden.

"And I keep getting the same recorded message—that their cell phone is turned off."

Reverend Camden shrugged. "Maybe it is."

Mrs. Camden shot him an annoyed look. "That's all you can say?"

"Well, honey, we agreed to trust them,

73

so let's trust them," he told her, speaking loudly over the noise in the hall. "I'm sure everything is fine."

Mrs. Camden made a face. "Well, I'm *not* so sure. I'm going to call my father and see if he's heard from them yet."

Simon loudly cleared his throat. He was standing next to Ruthie and his twin brothers, who were both fast asleep in their double stroller. Reverend and Mrs. Camden looked at their son.

"What?" they asked at the same time.

"You should have listened to *me*," Simon said, "then you'd *know* if something was wrong."

"How's that?" Reverend Camden asked.

"I'm the one member of this family who wanted to get a police radio for the electric van. If we had a police radio, then we'd know if there have been any major accidents on the highway."

Ruthie laughed and Mrs. Camden grew pale. Reverend Camden instantly guided Simon away from his mother.

"Come on," he said, "let's take a trip to the refreshment area."

"But I was just trying to help," Simon protested.

"I think we've had about enough of your 'help' for one day," Reverend Camden replied.

Mrs. Camden, meanwhile, frantically dialed her father's number. All she got was a busy signal.

"Hello, Grandpa Charles? This is Mary."

She pushed the phone close to her ear to shut out the noise at the rest stop.

"Hey, kiddo," Grandpa Charles said, brushing his mustache. "Ginger and I are expecting you here any minute."

"I know," Mary replied, "but we're behind schedule. We had car trouble."

"Nothing serious, I hope," Grandpa Charles said.

"Everything's all right now, but we're running a little behind schedule."

"No problem," Grandpa Charles said with a chuckle. "We'll keep the light on for you. Is there anything else we can do for you?"

"Maybe," Mary said. "If Mom or Dad calls, could you sort of, well . . ."

"Cover for you? Sure I can. I know how your mom frets. Annie always was a worrier."

Mary breathed a sigh of relief.

"Thanks, Grandpa. We'll see you in a few hours."

Mary hung up just as Lucy arrived.

"I told him we'd be late," Mary said.

Lucy reached for the pay phone. "I'm going to call Mom and Dad."

Mary grabbed her sister's arm "Oh, no you're not."

"Why?"

"Because they will ask a lot of questions I'm not prepared to answer," Mary replied. "And neither are you."

"Fine," Lucy said. "Then let's get back on the road."

Sandi was waiting for them in the minivan. She had been looking through Grandpa Charles's memory album.

"Is this your family?" she asked.

Mary nodded as she sat in the backseat next to the girl. Lucy got behind the wheel.

"That's Matt, our older brother. And there are Simon and Ruthie," Mary said. "Those two are the newest Camdens—twin boys. And this is Happy, the world's most annoying dog."

"I have an older brother, too," Sandi

told them. "He's in the Marine Corps, stationed in Japan. I hardly ever see him."

"Do you have any other brothers or sisters?"

"I've got a little brother named Tommy," Sandi replied. "He's the shining star of our family unit."

Mary and Lucy both detected a note of bitterness in Sandi's voice.

"What about your father and mother?" said Mary.

"My mom died," Sandi said without emotion.

"I'm sorry," Mary said softly.

"It happened a long time ago," Sandi replied with a shrug. "Right after Tommy was born. I hardly remember my mother."

Then Sandi smiled again.

"Weren't those motorcycles something!"

"Did you ever ride a motorcycle?" Mary asked. "Back home, I mean?"

"No, but I love them. I love fast cars, big trucks, *and* motorcycles. Someday I want to own a Harley. When I'm rich and famous."

"I like motorcycles, too," Mary confessed. "But with school and basketball and stuff, I never had time to learn to drive one."

"I like sports, too," Sandi said. "My little brother calls me a tomboy."

"What does your dad say?" Lucy asked.

Sandi frowned. "My dad doesn't understand. He wants me to like girl things, but I don't. And he hates my nose candy."

"Your what?"

Sandi tapped the little jewel on her nose with her finger.

"My pierced nose. My dad says it's not ladylike, but I don't care."

"Sounds like you pretty much do what you want," Lucy said.

"Pretty much," said Sandi. "My dad thinks I'm nothing but trouble. He says I dyed my hair orange just so he couldn't call me the black sheep of the family anymore."

In the rearview mirror, Mary and Lucy exchanged glances.

"Tell us more about your dad and your family," Lucy said. But Sandi only wanted to talk about the Heaven's Angels.

"That's what I want to do," Sandi said with a wistful sigh. "Live free on the road, with a fast set of wheels and no family or responsibilities. Or maybe I'll go to New York and start an all-girl hip-hop band."

She looked at Mary, then at Lucy.

"That's the great thing about being on the road, without any ties to hold you back," she said. "You're free to do *what* you want to do, *when* you want to do it."

"Well, I finally got through to Dad and Ginger," Mrs. Camden announced as she sat down at the conference table. "Dad told me that Mary and Lucy just called him from a rest stop to say that they are almost there."

The news was positive, but Reverend Camden saw that his wife wasn't smiling.

"Dad couldn't get off the phone fast enough, and Ginger refused to even talk to me," she told him.

Then Mrs. Camden frowned. "There's something fishy going on, and I think we should get to the bottom of it."

Reverend Camden nodded. "Maybe," he told her. "But let's give it some time. The break's over and the conference program is about to resume."

Matt felt like he'd been walking for hours. The knapsack felt like a lead weight on his back, and his feet ached.

"I've got to be close to the highway now," he said out loud, just to hear a human voice. It had been over an hour since he'd even seen a car go by.

He looked ahead and stopped in his tracks.

"The policeman didn't say anything about a fork in the road!" he moaned. "Now there are two roads in front of me. How am I supposed to know which one to take?"

There were no signs, no directions of any kind. Just two roads that went off in separate directions.

Matt sighed and eased the pack off his back. He was tired, thirsty, hungry, and penniless.

"Not to mention lost." He finished his thought out loud with a sigh.

The sun was hot, so he trudged into a line of trees and sat down in the shade. He immediately noticed that the shadows were getting longer, which meant daylight was fading fast.

"I better find civilization before it gets too dark," he mumbled.

But first he had to pick a road.

"I'll flip a coin," he decided. "Except that I don't have any coins left. Maybe I'll just flag somebody down and ask directions."

Matt leaned against the thick trunk of a tree. Then he yawned and closed his eyes.

"Just a short rest while I wait for somebody to drive by," he muttered to himself as he drifted off to sleep.

The sound of driving was hypnotic.

Sandi became sleepy and started to lean on Mary's shoulder.

"Why don't you just lie down all the way?" asked Mary. She crawled over the front seat and sat next to Lucy so Sandi could stretch out in the back.

Soon, Sandi was fast asleep.

Mary glanced back at the girl and wondered if friction between her and her father had caused Sandi to run away from home.

"Do you think she's in trouble?" Mary asked.

Eyes on the road, Lucy shrugged.

"Maybe it's not family trouble," Mary said. "Maybe it's boy trouble."

Lucy nodded. "Could be. Girls get into an awful lot of trouble because of boys."

"Some girls do," Mary said smugly. "But not me."

Lucy chuckled. "No, of course not *you.*"

"What's that supposed to mean?" Mary demanded.

"Nothing personal," Lucy replied. "I just meant that we've both had our share of boy trouble in the past."

"Nothing we couldn't handle."

"I know how to handle boys," Lucy replied. "But sometimes I'm not so sure about you."

"Now I'm starting to get mad," Mary said, only half-seriously.

"Well, it's true," Lucy insisted. "You're not the best judge of character, you know."

"Hah," Mary snorted. "You forget. I'm your sister. I know all about you. *And* your boyfriends. With one exception, they were all a bunch of losers."

"One exception?"

"Jordan," Mary said emphatically. "He was your only good boyfriend."

"You should know," Lucy shot back. "You stole him from me."

Mary's eyes went wide. "I did not! I'm not a boyfriend stealer!"

"Well, maybe *stole* is too strong a word," Lucy said. "Let's just say I *found* him for you."

Mary was starting to get angry for real now.

"I don't need you to find boys for me, *little sister*."

In the backseat, Sandi stirred. But neither Mary nor Lucy noticed.

"Oh, no?" Lucy shot back. "Maybe you only need me if you want to find winners instead of *losers*."

"Hey," Mary said, folding her arms over her chest. "If you want to talk losers, let's talk about your ex-boyfriend Jimmy Moon."

It was Lucy's turn to get mad.

"There is nothing wrong with Jimmy Moon. After we broke up, he just got into a little trouble, that's all."

"You call drug possession 'a little trouble'?"

"He wasn't *doing* drugs," Lucy cried. "He just got caught with some other guys who *did*. It was guilt by association. Like you and your trailer park friends."

Mary sat up. "That was a mistake. I had no idea they'd pull out a marijuana joint."

But Lucy dug deeper. "It's not like he's an ex-con or something."

As soon as she spoke, Lucy regretted it. But it was too late to take it back.

"What!" Mary cried. "Are you saying Jimmy Moon wasn't an ex-con, but Robbie and I *are?*"

"No!" Lucy said. "I wasn't saying that at all. You know what I—"

"*Don't* talk to me," Mary said angrily, turning away.

"But—"

"Look! There's a rest stop," Mary announced, pointing to the road ahead. "Pull over. *Now!* I need some air. Some *fresh* air. It's too close for comfort in here. . . ."

TEN

The rumble of an approaching cement truck shook Matt awake. He jumped to his feet when he saw the truck barreling down the road. He ran between the trees, waving his hands at the lumbering vehicle.

But Matt was too slow. The truck passed before he could even get to the road.

He watched as the truck took the left fork and disappeared into the distance. He rubbed the dust out of his eyes and looked up at the sky.

It was late afternoon. *Very* late.

Matt ran back to the tree, snatched up his backpack, and walked toward the left fork in the road.

"That truck must have been heading for the highway, right?" Matt reasoned aloud with himself. "And I've been walking a long time, so I have to be pretty close to the highway now, right?"

Matt frowned. "Now all I have to figure out is what I do once I actually *get* to the highway."

Lucy barely had time to stop before Mary jumped out of the minivan. Lucy cut the engine, grabbed the keys, and ran after her.

"Mary, wait!" she cried. "I'm sorry for what I said."

"Leave me alone!" Mary screamed.

She crossed the parking lot and walked toward the comfort station.

Lucy soon caught up with her.

"Come on, Mary. Talk to me."

Mary tried to walk away, but Lucy grabbed her arm. Mary yanked it away so hard she stumbled over the curb and landed on her backside.

"Ouch!" she howled.

"Are you okay?"

"No."

"Let me help you," Lucy said, offering

Mary her hand. Mary brushed it away.

"First you insult me. Now you want to help?"

Lucy nodded. "Exactly. That's what I'm here for."

"What?" Mary huffed, brushing the hair away from her face. "To insult me?"

"No," Lucy replied. "To *help* you. That's what sisters are for. That's what *families* are for."

Mary took her sister's hand. "Then stop judging me! Do you know how sick I am of being judged?"

"Look," Lucy said as Mary dusted herself off. "Everybody does stupid things. Everybody falls down. Nobody's perfect, and I was stupid and wrong to say what I said."

Mary nodded. "I agree."

"But," Lucy continued, "I can't go back in time and change the things you did. Trashing the school and the probation and the drinking and lying. Those things happened, and they were wrong."

"I know I did bad things, but—"

"—but I promise you that I will never let the past come between us," Lucy told her. "And you have to promise me that you'll be a little less sensitive about the past, or you'll never get to the future."

Mary frowned. "My little sister giving *me* advice. What's wrong with this picture?"

Then Mary shook her head. "But do you know what's really sad? In lots of people's eyes, I *am* just an ex-con."

"Not to the people who *count*," Lucy said, smiling. "Not to me, or Matt, or Simon, or Ruthie. To all of us, you're our *sister* . . . and that will always be more important."

Lucy's smile turned teasing. "Our big, dumb, clumsy sister who trips over her own huge feet."

"You pushed me," Mary said, smiling, too.

"No way! You tripped over those gigantic dogs of yours."

Then they both started to laugh. The anger and hurt disappeared, and once again they were sisters. They laughed until they got back to the minivan.

It was empty.

Sandi, the runaway they were so determined to help, was *gone*.

* * *

Matt trudged up a long hill, his feet aching with each step. At the top, he was hoping to see the highway. But when he got there, all he saw were acres and acres of plowed fields, trees, and the mountains beyond.

Matt had chosen the wrong fork in the road.

He eased the pack off his shoulders and leaned against a tree. Then he looked up at the sky. The sun was ready to disappear behind the horizon. It would soon be dark.

"That's it," Matt said out loud. "I'm done for today."

With the backpack dangling from his grip, Matt moved halfway down the hill, until he saw a rocky cliff in an area surrounded by trees. It appeared as good a place as any to spend the night. There was shelter under the trees, and his back was against the hill. If the weather turned ugly, he could always huddle against the cliff.

Matt dropped to the ground and pulled off his shoes. He rubbed his tired feet. Then he stretched out, using his pack as a pillow.

He felt itchy for a minute, until he got used to lying on the bare ground.

His stomach rumbled.

"This wouldn't be so bad if I had something to eat," he murmured.

Just then, something plopped on the ground near Matt's head. He sat up and squinted into the deepening gloom.

A shiny red apple was lying on the ground. Matt was sure it wasn't there before. Then he looked closer at the branches of the trees overhead.

They were heavy with apples. Hundreds and hundreds of apples. He was in an orchard!

Grabbing the fallen apple, Matt rubbed it against his shirt and took a big bite. It was a little sour, but Matt found it delicious.

He gobbled the rest of it down. Then he put on his shoes and went in search of more.

Before Matt took his first bite out of a second apple, he turned his eyes to the sky.

"Thank you," he said.

"We have to find Sandi," Mary said frantically. "We *have* to!"

"Don't panic," Lucy replied. "She can't have gone far. There's nobody else here, so she couldn't have bummed another ride."

Mary's eyes were haunted. "It's all my fault. Me and my stupid feelings. She probably heard us fighting and got annoyed."

"Probably," Lucy said. "But that doesn't matter now. We just have to find her."

Together they searched the rest rooms, the pay phones, and the picnic area.

Finally they found Sandi sitting on a picnic bench, her head down. She was hugging the memory album.

"Sandi?" Mary said. "Is something wrong?"

The girl jumped at the sound of Mary's voice. Tears were streaming down her face.

"Wha-what's wrong?" Mary asked.

"I . . . I want to go home," Sandi gasped between sobs.

Mary took the girl in her arms and hugged her. Sandi leaned against her and cried.

A moment later, it began to rain.

Mary led Sandi back to the minivan.

"I'm so sorry," Sandi sobbed. "All you wanted to do was see your grandfather, and I—"

Now it was Lucy who spoke.

"You didn't do anything wrong," she said. "Let's get dry, and then we'll take you home. No matter what, we'll get you back to your family."

ELEVEN

Tossing away the last apple core, Matt rubbed his stomach and burped. Then he stretched out under the trees, his back to the hillside.

The night was cool but not cold. Using his jacket for a blanket and the backpack for a pillow, Matt was fairly comfortable.

In the morning, he would retrace his steps and find his way back to the fork in the road. Hopefully, he would find the highway soon after that.

"Maybe I can still get to Mountain View in time for the music festival," he told himself.

Matt was almost asleep when the first

raindrop hit his forehead. He opened his eyes.

In a few minutes, the drizzle became a steady rain. Matt rose and huddled against the shelter of the cliff to keep dry.

It almost worked, but Matt knew he was in for a very wet night. He pulled the jacket up over his head and tried to sleep.

Back at the minivan, Sandi wiped her eyes as Mary dug through her luggage for some dry clothes for all of them.

As they dried themselves off and changed, Sandi told them why she ran away from home.

"It was so stupid and it was all my fault," she began.

"My dad had to go out of town because my aunt was real sick. He left me in charge of my little brother, Tommy.

"My dad was only supposed to be gone for a day or two."

Sandi frowned. "But after a few days, my dad called and said he had to stay with Aunt May another day or two. When I told Tommy, he began to cry. No matter what I did, he just wouldn't shut up.

"Finally I promised to take him to a

pizza parlor. He hadn't been out of the house in a couple of days and he was really getting restless. He's just a kid, you know?"

"I know," Mary said. "I have a bunch just like him at home."

"Well," Sandi sniffed, "to get to the pizza place, I had to drive. But I don't have a license yet, only a permit. I'm not allowed to drive without an adult in the car.

"Even worse, my dad told me never to drive his pickup truck. He makes his living with that truck, and if something happened to it, we'd probably starve or something.

"But Dad drove the car to our aunt's house, so the pickup truck was all I had."

Sandi wiped her eyes with the sleeve of her sweatshirt.

"Tommy wouldn't stop crying, and he wanted pizza, so I thought what's the harm, right? He gets his pizza and we go home, end of story."

Her eyes became haunted.

"Only the story didn't end that way, because that's not what happened."

Sandi started to cry again. "I drove so carefully. But on the way back from the pizza place, a car hit us at an intersection.

"One second we were just sitting there, talking and waiting for the light to turn green. The next second—"

Sandi paused. "There was a crash and glass was flying everywhere, and suddenly the truck was on its side and I was tangled up in the seat belt."

"But you were okay, right?" Lucy said anxiously.

"I was," Sandi replied. "But when I looked at Tommy—"

Sandi began to sob. "He was so pale. . . . And there was blood and glass, and I could smell gasoline, and I was afraid we'd both burn up. . . ."

Lucy gave Sandi a tissue so she could wipe her nose.

"Then the ambulance came, and they took Tommy to the hospital. The police came, too, and they told me the driver who hit us was drunk. But it didn't matter because I was in trouble, too, 'cause I didn't have a license."

"What about Tommy?"

"I saw him in the hospital later. He had a head injury and was unconscious, and the doctors weren't sure if he was okay or not. They said he might be okay, but he might not, and they wouldn't know until he woke up and they didn't know when that would be.

"And then the police called my dad. He told them he was coming back right away and then they put me on the phone with him."

"Was he upset?" Mary asked softly.

"He . . . he just started yelling at me. Saying that I killed my little brother and that I was always trouble and he was ashamed to have me as a daughter."

Sandi wiped her eyes.

"When I hung up, I asked the policeman if I could go to the bathroom. When I came out, the policeman's back was turned, so I left the hospital and ran away.

"That was three days ago. I tried to call the hospital a couple of times—but I never had enough money for long distance. Then I spent the little bit I had on food, and so I don't even know if my little brother is alive or dead."

Tears welled up in her eyes. "I've been alone and hungry and scared ever since I ran away. I've been hitchhiking, going back and forth, not sure where I should go but never going too far from home 'cause I guess I really want to go back. . . . I just didn't know how."

"We're going to take you back, right now," Mary told her.

"To what?" Sandi cried. "For all I know, my little brother could be . . ." Her voice trailed off. "And anyway," Sandi continued, "after what I did to Tommy, my dad probably hates me."

"People get mad and say stupid things. And do stupid things," Lucy told her. "I'm sure your dad was probably just crazy with worry and said a lot of things he didn't mean."

"Yeah," Mary said. "And right now, your dad is probably crazy with worry over *you*."

Sandi rolled her eyes. "But I disobeyed my dad and I hurt my little brother. I wrecked his truck, I ruined his life—"

"No," Mary cried. "Don't *ever* say that. The only mistake you made was running away instead of staying around to face the consequences of your mistake."

"But how can my dad ever forgive me?" Sandi asked, her eyes glistening.

"Because you are his daughter and he

loves you more than anything," Mary said. "That's something that will never change. No matter what you do, no matter what he says."

"He still loves me?" Sandi asked doubtfully.

"Yes," Mary told her. "And you can trust me, because I *know*. I made big mistakes, too. I did terrible things. I hurt my parents, my brothers and sisters, even my friends.

"But you know what? My parents love me, anyway. And so do my brothers and sisters. And all of them stayed right by my side through all the really bad consequences of my stupid actions."

Mary paused. "And do you know what? They never, *ever* gave up on me."

Mary looked at Lucy, her eyes asking for help.

Lucy nodded and said, "I'm sure your dad loves you, too. And I'm sure your dad would never give up on you, either. You just have to give him a chance to prove that to you."

The three of them sat in silence for a long time, listening to the rain pattering on the roof of the minivan.

Finally, Lucy spoke. "Well," she said, "we've got a gassed-up minivan. And we've got this lovely night for driving. So where to?"

Sandi thought about it for a little while.

"I . . . I live in a little town called Pine Ridge. It's not too far from here," she said at last.

"Okay." Mary smiled. "Let's find Pine Ridge on the map."

Sleep was impossible. Matt was soaked to the skin. He could feel cold rain running down his back and water squishing around in his shoes. And the rain just kept on coming.

Matt had just about decided that things couldn't get worse, when they did.

It began with a roaring sound, like a waterfall far, far away. But it soon got closer. He figured out what the noise was just seconds before a wall of water came washing over him.

Gallons of brown muddy water poured down the hill, lifting Matt off the ground and washing him over the rise.

Matt grasped for his backpack, and his

fingers just touched it before he—along with his pack—went careening down the hillside.

He tried to fight the tide of slime, but it was impossible. He felt like he was riding a barrel over Niagara Falls, only there was no barrel. There was just him.

He rolled over and over, bouncing off trees and shooting over rocks until he was able to reach out and grab a thick root sticking out of the ground.

Dragging himself to the nearest tree, he hugged the trunk. Mud and water poured over him.

Under the steady impact of the water, Matt felt his shoes pull away from his feet. He clutched the tree with white knuckles.

Then Matt heard the thunder and saw the flash of lightning.

Then it *really* started to rain!

TWELVE

It was almost nine o'clock when Lucy stopped the minivan in front of a tiny brick house on a quiet suburban street in the little town of Pine Ridge.

In the front yard, she saw a swing set, a sliding board, and a little cactus growing by the fence.

"We're here," Lucy announced.

"Home, sweet home," Sandi mumbled.

Her face was pale, her lips trembling. But she didn't hesitate. Sandi opened the door and stepped onto the sidewalk.

The light on the front porch came on.

A moment later, a heavyset man with a thick black beard opened the door.

"Daddy," Sandi said softly.

"Sandi!" the man cried, pushing through the door. "Is that you? Is that really you!"

The girl ran into her father's arms.

"Daddy, Daddy," Sandi sobbed. "I'm so sorry."

"No, I'm the one who's sorry for those terrible things I said to you. I was so worried! Where were you?"

Sandi could hardly speak, he was hugging her so tightly.

"Oh, Sandi, I was sick with worry. We both were. . . ."

"Both?" Sandi asked with hope.

Just then, a little boy in pajamas came to the door. He had a thick bandage on his head.

"Is that you, sis?" the boy asked sleepily.

"Tommy!" Sandi cried. "You're okay."

Tommy ran up to Sandi and hugged her legs. "I missed you, Sandi," he said.

"Tommy is just fine," Sandi's father told her. "He was out of the hospital in two days."

Then he looked down at his daughter. "But how are you? I was so worried. I thought you were gone for good. I thought

I'd lost my little girl. . . ."

"I'm sorry I wrecked your truck," Sandi sobbed.

"I can always buy another truck," he told her. "But where am I going to find another daughter?"

"According to this map, we still have to drive about an hour before we get to Phoenix," Mary said.

"Then I guess we have a lot of explaining to do," said Lucy with a smile.

Mary nodded. She was smiling, too.

"I mean, think about it. What *didn't* we do wrong?" Lucy cried.

"Yeah," Mary said. "We picked up a hitchhiker. We ran out of gas. We hooked up with a motorcycle gang. We drove miles and miles out of our way. . . ."

"Yep," Lucy said, "we're definitely going to get it."

"But you know what?" Mary replied. "I don't care what Mom and Dad do to us. I think we did the right thing."

"Me too," said Lucy. "And that's all that really matters, right?"

Mary nodded. "Right. Be true to yourself and all that."

"Yeah," Lucy said, "we did good."

"Now," Mary said with a sigh, "all we have to do is convince Mom and Dad that we did the right thing. . . ."

"Sure," Lucy said brightly, "how hard is that?"

Then they both frowned.

"We're toast," said Mary.

Even though they arrived very late, Mary and Lucy had a wonderful night visiting with their grandfather and his wife, Ginger. The first thing they did was call their parents, who were relieved to know they were safe.

But before Mrs. Camden could get a full explanation out of them, Grandpa Charles took the phone away and scolded Annie for taking precious time away from him and his granddaughters.

Mary and Lucy exchanged glances. What a relief!

The older couple laid out a big spread of leftovers from Grandpa Charles's birthday dinner, including big hunks of chocolate cake. Then the girls sat down at the table and talked about their crazy road trip, including picking up the runaway girl and getting her back to her family.

Grandpa Charles was impressed with how they had helped the girl.

After dinner the girls proudly presented their grandfather with the memory album. Together they paged through the thick book.

"Do you remember this?" Mary asked, pointing at a faded picture of a cabin by a lake.

"Oh, yes, I do, kiddo," Grandpa Charles replied. "That was the summer we all went up to Oregon together!"

"Is that me?" Lucy laughed, pointing to a picture of Mrs. Camden holding a chubby baby.

"Your grandmother loved that cabin," Grandpa Charles told them. "We ended up spending three summers in a row up there."

"And here's a picture of Matt," Mary said, pointing to a skinny kid in an over-sized bathing suit.

"My, that suit's falling off him," Ginger said.

"If I remember correctly, it *did* fall off," Grandpa Charles said, chuckling.

"That's right!" Mary howled.

"Matt was always getting himself into a fix," said Grandpa Charles. "I'll bet he still is."

"Not anymore," Lucy said. "He's pretty responsible these days."

"Yeah," Grandpa Charles said with a twinkle in his eye. "I'll bet."

"Oh, Grandpa," Lucy said.

"Hey, here's a new picture of Lucy, Ruthie, and Simon," Mary said. "Pretty good, huh? I took this picture myself."

"My, that Ruthie's cute," Grandpa Charles said. "But what happened to Simon's hair? It's getting pretty long. He's not going to end up like Matt, is he?"

"It's the newest fashion," Lucy said.

"I think it looks downright silly," Grandpa Charles replied. "But the dog looks well groomed. Her name is Happy, isn't it?"

"Yes," said Mary with a smile, exchanging proud glances with her sister. Mary knew they had done a good thing for their grandfather coming here—and it *felt* good.

The morning came too quickly. After a nice long breakfast visit, they packed up the minivan for the trip back.

"We're really sorry this visit was so short. We didn't mean for it to take so long to get here," Lucy said.

"Yes," Mary agreed, hugging her grandfather, "but we had a great time."

"Think nothing of it," Grandpa Charles told them. "You did the right thing, and I'm proud of you. You may have saved that girl, er—"

"Sandi."

"—Sandi's life."

"Thanks, Grandpa," said Mary and Lucy together.

"Thank you, girls. Especially for the memory album. I know it will help me." Grandpa Charles grinned as he hugged the girls. "Come back soon," he said.

"We will," they promised, then climbed back into the minivan.

Mary and Lucy weren't on the road for ten minutes before Mrs. Camden called Grandpa Charles.

"Why didn't Mary and Lucy call us before they left!" Mrs. Camden cried.

"Now, Annie, they called you last night and told you they got in safe. Stop your worrying."

"But I still haven't got my explanation as to why they took so long driving to Phoenix! And why they turned off their cell phone!"

"I think you should calm down now, Annie. Like I told you last night, they said they wanted to wait to talk to you. They want to explain everything in person—"

"You know, Dad, I was hoping that you would talk some sense into those girls. They *are* your granddaughters."

"They *have* sense, Annie," Grandpa Charles replied. "More sense than you know."

"What do you mean?" Mrs. Camden exclaimed.

"Look, honey," Grandpa Charles said, "I know the girls wanted to explain it all to you in their own way. But I can see how angry you are—so I think maybe you should hear this news first from me. Just put Eric on the other extension, and then I'll tell you both a story about two daughters any parent would be proud to have."

THIRTEEN

Matt slept very late.

No big surprise, since he'd been exhausted from his near-drowning the night before!

By the time he opened his eyes, the sun was high in the sky. Immediately he began to search for his lost shoes and backpack.

Though the rain had stopped hours before dawn, Matt's clothes were still damp and caked with mud.

He was itchy and uncomfortable, and he wanted nothing more than to get out of his filthy clothes.

He finally found his pack. Then he found his right shoe. He searched and searched, but never found the other one.

He drew his spare pair from the back-pack and put them on.

During his search, Matt found a water pump and washed the mud off. Then he changed into fresh clothes from his pack. They were damp, but at least they weren't too muddy.

By eleven o'clock, he had retraced his steps to the fork in the road. Five minutes later, he spotted a car.

Figuring he had no other choice, Matt violated one of his own rules of the road.

He stuck out his thumb.

The car slowed and stopped.

"Matthew Camden!" the driver said. "I can't believe it. What a coincidence."

"Bill . . . Bill Tully?" Matt cried, greeting his friend from college.

"John Hamilton was wondering where you were," Bill said. "We gave up on you."

"Well, here I am," Matt said, climbing into the car beside the driver. "And I'm all ready to go to Mountain View."

"Sorry, man," Bill Tully replied. "It's my mom's birthday and I'm going to visit my parents."

Matt's shoulders sagged.

"If you want, I can take you to the

highway where you can bum a ride to
Mountain View," Bill told him. "Everybody's up there waiting for you. It's a real
blast."

Matt thought about it.

He *could* hitch a ride to Mountain
View. He might be able to salvage a little of
his weekend getaway, after all.

"Where do your folks live?" Matt asked.

"Real close to the college," Bill replied.
"Less than fifty miles from Glenoak, actually."

*Glenoak and home? Or my thumb, the
highway, and a trip to who-knows-where?*

It wasn't a tough decision.

"Drop me off as close to Glenoak as
you can get," Matt replied. "I just want to
go home."

Mary flipped the cell phone open, then
flipped it closed again.

From behind the wheel of the minivan,
Lucy shot her sister a look. "If you want
to use that thing, we should get fresh
batteries."

"What?" Mary cried. "And have it ring?
And then have to answer it, only to hear
Mom's or Dad's—or Mom's *and* Dad's

voices on the other end of the line demand-
ing to know what happened and how we
are going to pay and pay?"

Lucy shivered theatrically. "Whew,
you've got a point. But we do have to face
them soon. We're only twenty miles from
home."

"A lot can happen in twenty miles,"
Mary replied.

"Yeah!" Lucy cried, her eyes wide.
"Like you can see your older brother standing on the side of the road with his thumb
out like he's trying to hitch a ride."

"Unlikely," Mary said. "But I guess it's
possible."

"More than possible," Lucy cried,
pointing to the road ahead. "Look!"

"Boy!" Matt cried, waving his arms
frantically. "Am I ever glad to see you!"

As the minivan rolled by, Mary stuck
her head out of the open window.

"Sorry," she cried. "My older brother
told me *never* to pick up a hitchhiker."

Matt's jaw dropped as the minivan
sped away.

"Stop," he cried, running after them.
"Please stop!"

Mary and Lucy howled with laughter.

"Wha . . . what should we do?" Mary said between giggles.

"I'll circle around and pick the poor guy up," Lucy replied, unable to stop laughing.

"Did you see the look on Matt's face?" she cried.

They were still giggling when they finally pulled up beside him.

Reverend and Mrs. Camden were waiting for Mary and Lucy in the kitchen.

If they were surprised to see Matt with the girls, they didn't show it. They waited for their daughters to speak.

Mary and Lucy walked up to their parents and looked them in the eye.

"Mom. Dad," Lucy began. "We . . . we have something to tell you—"

"To confess, actually," Mary added.

"We . . . ," said Lucy.

"I . . . ," said Mary.

Mrs. Camden threw her arms around Mary and then Lucy.

"We're so proud of you! Both of you," Reverend Camden said.

"Huh?"

"Grandpa Charles told us all about it,"

Reverend Camden explained. "He says he hopes you're not mad at him for telling us, but he couldn't stand us being mad at you."

"He is really proud of you," Mrs. Camden said. "And so am I."

"I'm not sure you did everything right," Reverend Camden said. "But whatever you did seemed to work out for the best."

"It worked out perfectly," Mrs. Camden said.

"I talked to Sandi's father this morning," Reverend Camden told them.

"How?" Mary cried.

"No great mystery," Reverend Camden told her. "Sandi got our phone number from directory assistance, and she called us to explain what happened."

"Yes," Mrs. Camden added, "he was very grateful, to both of you."

"Well," Reverend Camden said, "I hope you won't make a habit of picking up strangers. But this time, I'm glad you did."

"Wait a minute! This is crazy," Matt cried. "Mary and Lucy break every safety regulation in the book, and you're *congratulating* them?"

"That reminds me," Reverend Camden

said. "A nice mechanic from Glenoak Garage called this morning. He said your Camaro also needs a new carburetor as well as a fuel pump."

Matt frowned.

"He also said that all your car trouble could have been avoided if you'd taken better care of your engine. Just routine maintenance, he told me. Right, dear?"

Mrs. Camden nodded her head. "That's what the mechanic said. He sounded very knowledgeable."

"Next time, take care of your car," Reverend Camden said. "And you won't have to bum a ride home from . . . uh . . . *strangers*."

Matt's eyebrow rose, and his two sisters did their level best not to laugh again.

But they failed!

DON'T MISS THIS BRAND-NEW, ORIGINAL 7TH HEAVEN STORY

Coming June 2003!

MARY'S
RESCUE

Jennifer.

Mary Camden is working as a lifeguard at a fabulous beach resort, and she's invited her siblings to visit her. What could be more perfect? But this idyllic resort town holds secrets. . . . First, Mary's friend disappears from the beach on her watch. Then Mary gets blamed for a burglary. Can the Camden kids get to the bottom of these mysteries and clear Mary's name?

Coming June 2003!
ISBN: 0-375-82409-X

Based on the hit TV Show!

Jennifer

When Lucy gets back her wedding photos, it brings back memories. Now 7th Heaven fans can find out all the juicy details of Lucy's crazy and hectic wedding day.

RHCB

DON'T MISS THIS BRAND-NEW, ORIGINAL 7ᵀᴴ HEAVEN STORY.

Jennifer

Now Available!

LEARNING THE ROPES

Lucy goes to Washington! Her student court group has a date to be shown around the nation's capital for an entire weekend by an important politician. But she quickly learns that politicians aren't always that easy to get hold of. In the meantime, Simon wants to be an entrepreneur, so he decides to baby-sit for one of Ruthie's friends. But once Ruthie finds out Simon's plans, it seems Simon will have one more unexpected kid to look after. . . .

Available wherever books are sold!
ISBN: 0-375-81160-5